# GHOSTLY GRAPHIC ADVENTURES

# THE STAR ISLAND SPIRITS

Written by Baron Specter
Illustrated by Dustin Evans

magic wagon

Published by Magic Wagon, a division of the ABDO Group, 8000 West 78th Street, Edina, Minnesota 55439. Copyright © 2011 by Abdo Consulting Group, Inc. International copyrights reserved in all countries. All rights reserved. No part of this book may be reproduced in any form without written permission from the publisher.

Graphic Planet™ is a trademark and logo of Magic Wagon.

Printed in the United States of America, North Mankato, Minnesota.
052010
092010
♻This book contains at least 10% recycled materials.

Written by Baron Specter
Illustrated by Dustin Evans
Lettered and designed by Ardden Entertainment LLC
Edited by Stephanie Hedlund and Rochelle Baltzer
Cover art by Dustin Evans
Cover design by Ardden Entertainment LLC

## Library of Congress Cataloging-in-Publication Data

Specter, Baron, 1957-
   The fifth adventure : the Star Island spirits / by Baron Specter ;  illustrated by Dustin Evans.
      p. cm. --  (Ghostly graphic adventures)
   Summary: While searching for Blackbeard's treasure on Star Island, New Hampshire, Joey and Tank encounter the pirate ghosts that protect it.
   ISBN 978-1-60270-774-0
   1. Graphic novels. [1. Graphic novels. 2. Ghosts--Fiction. 3. Buried treasure--Fiction. 4. Pirates--Fiction. 5. Star Island (Rockingham County, N.H.)--Fiction.] I. Evans, Dustin, 1982- ill. II. Title. III. Title: Star Island spirits.
   PZ7.7.S648Fif 2010
   741.5'973--dc22
                                                                          2009052894

# TABLE OF CONTENTS

# OUR HEROES AND VILLAINS

 **Joey DeAngelo**
Hero

 **Blackbeard**
Villain

 **Tank**
Hero

 **1st Mate**
Villain

 **Mrs. DeAngelo**
Joey's Mom

 **Blackbeard's Wife**

 **Mitty**
Our Heroes' Helper

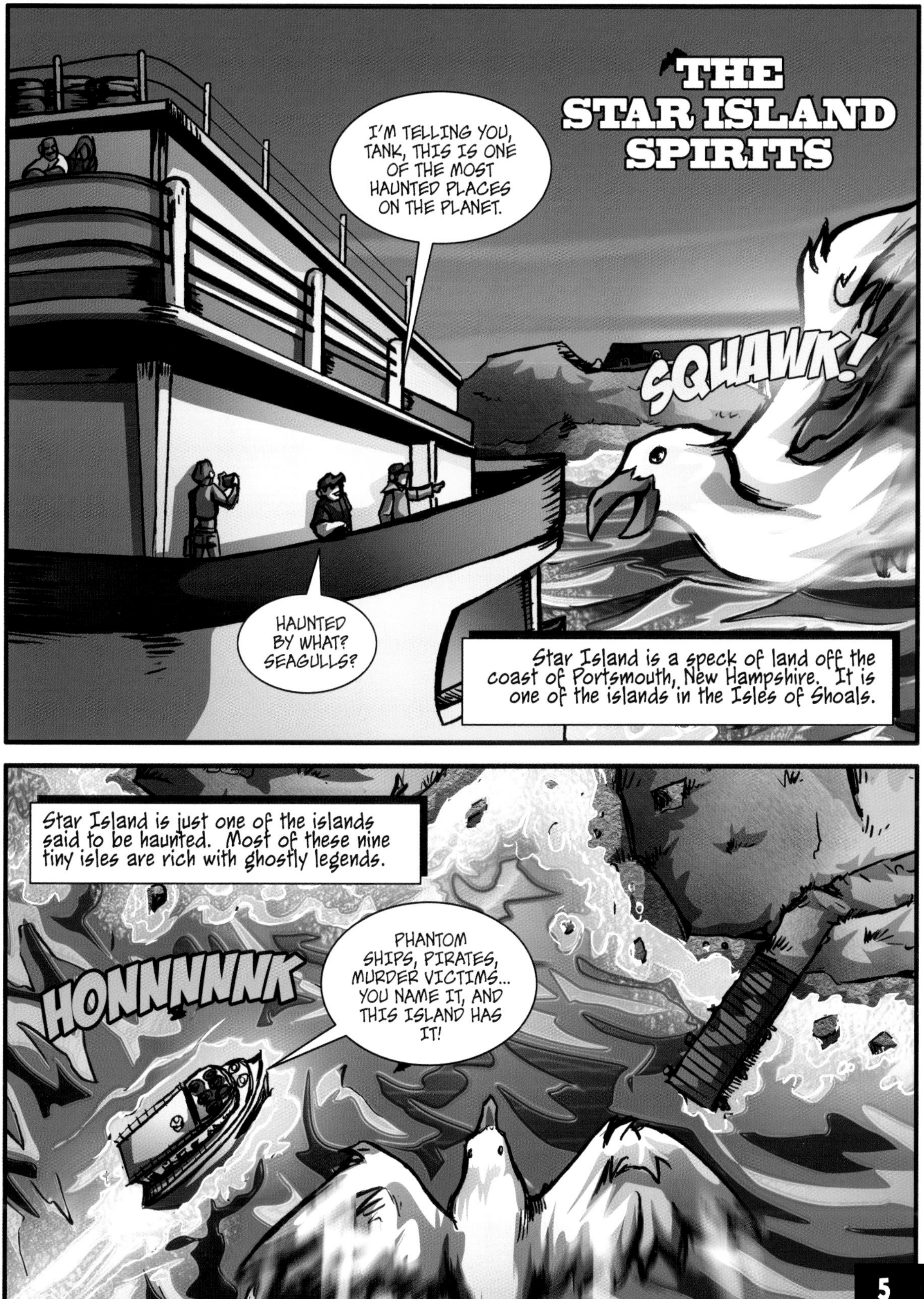
THE STAR ISLAND SPIRITS
I'M TELLING YOU, TANK, THIS IS ONE OF THE MOST HAUNTED PLACES ON THE PLANET.
HAUNTED BY WHAT? SEAGULLS?
SQUAWK!
Star Island is a speck of land off the coast of Portsmouth, New Hampshire. It is one of the islands in the Isles of Shoals.
Star Island is just one of the islands said to be haunted. Most of these nine tiny isles are rich with ghostly legends.
HONNNNNNK
PHANTOM SHIPS, PIRATES, MURDER VICTIMS... YOU NAME IT, AND THIS ISLAND HAS IT!

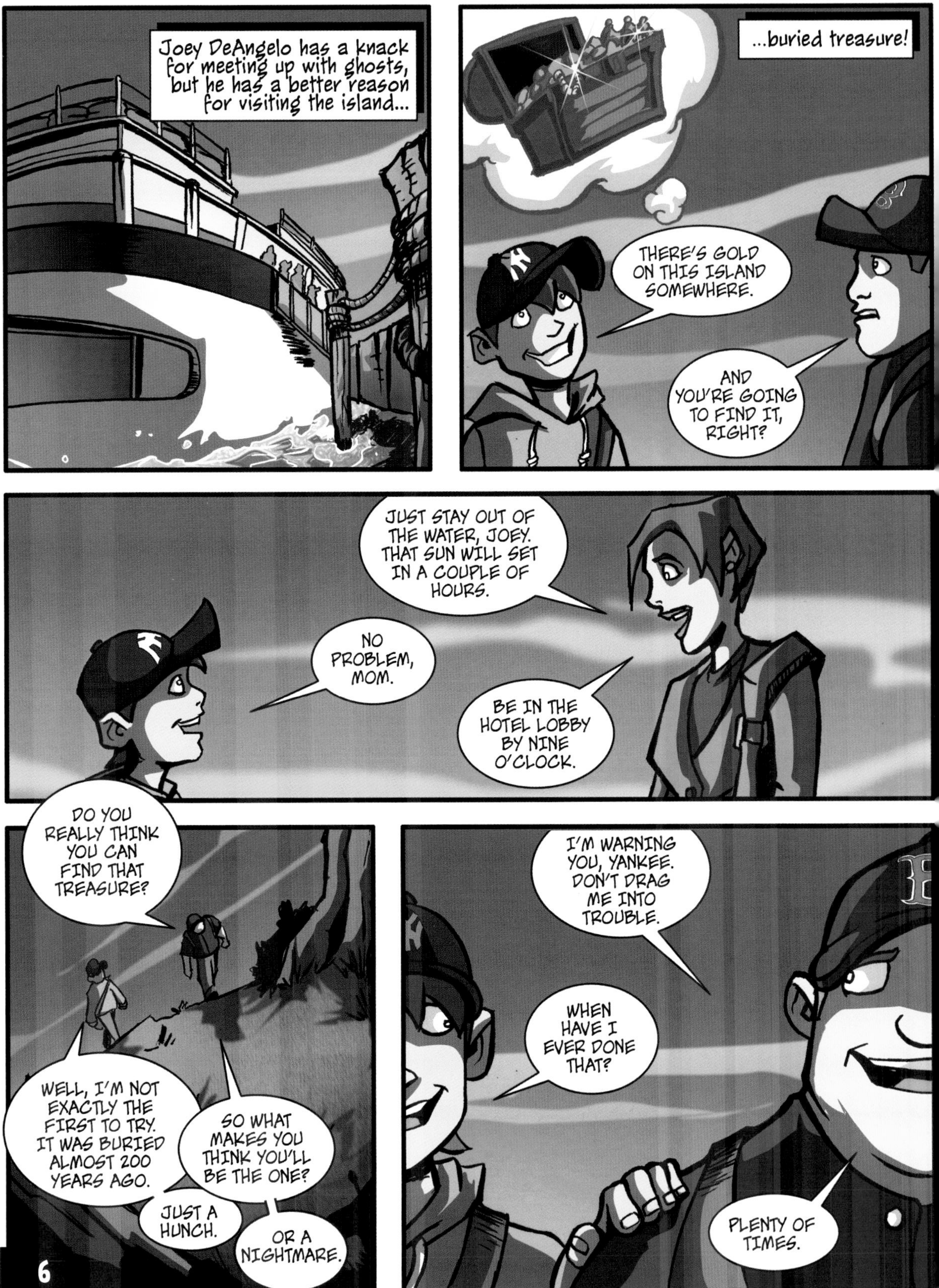
Joey DeAngelo has a knack for meeting up with ghosts, but he has a better reason for visiting the island...
...buried treasure!
THERE'S GOLD ON THIS ISLAND SOMEWHERE.
AND YOU'RE GOING TO FIND IT, RIGHT?
JUST STAY OUT OF THE WATER, JOEY. THAT SUN WILL SET IN A COUPLE OF HOURS.
NO PROBLEM, MOM.
BE IN THE HOTEL LOBBY BY NINE O'CLOCK.
DO YOU REALLY THINK YOU CAN FIND THAT TREASURE?
WELL, I'M NOT EXACTLY THE FIRST TO TRY. IT WAS BURIED ALMOST 200 YEARS AGO.
SO WHAT MAKES YOU THINK YOU'LL BE THE ONE?
JUST A HUNCH.
OR A NIGHTMARE.
I'M WARNING YOU, YANKEE. DON'T DRAG ME INTO TROUBLE.
WHEN HAVE I EVER DONE THAT?
PLENTY OF TIMES.

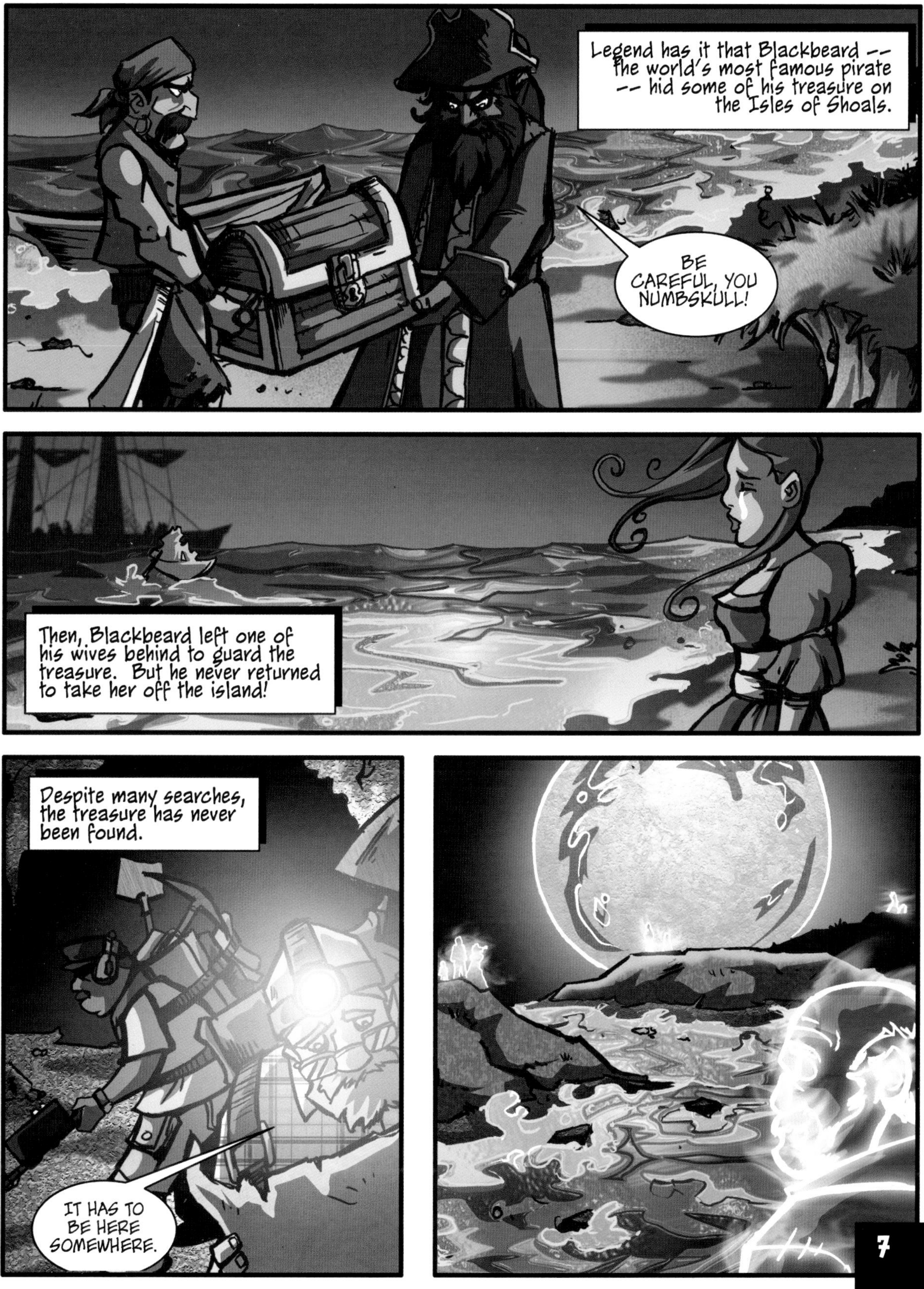

Legend has it that Blackbeard -- the world's most famous pirate -- hid some of his treasure on the Isles of Shoals.
BE CAREFUL, YOU NUMBSKULL!
Then, Blackbeard left one of his wives behind to guard the treasure. But he never returned to take her off the island!
Despite many searches, the treasure has never been found.
IT HAS TO BE HERE SOMEWHERE.

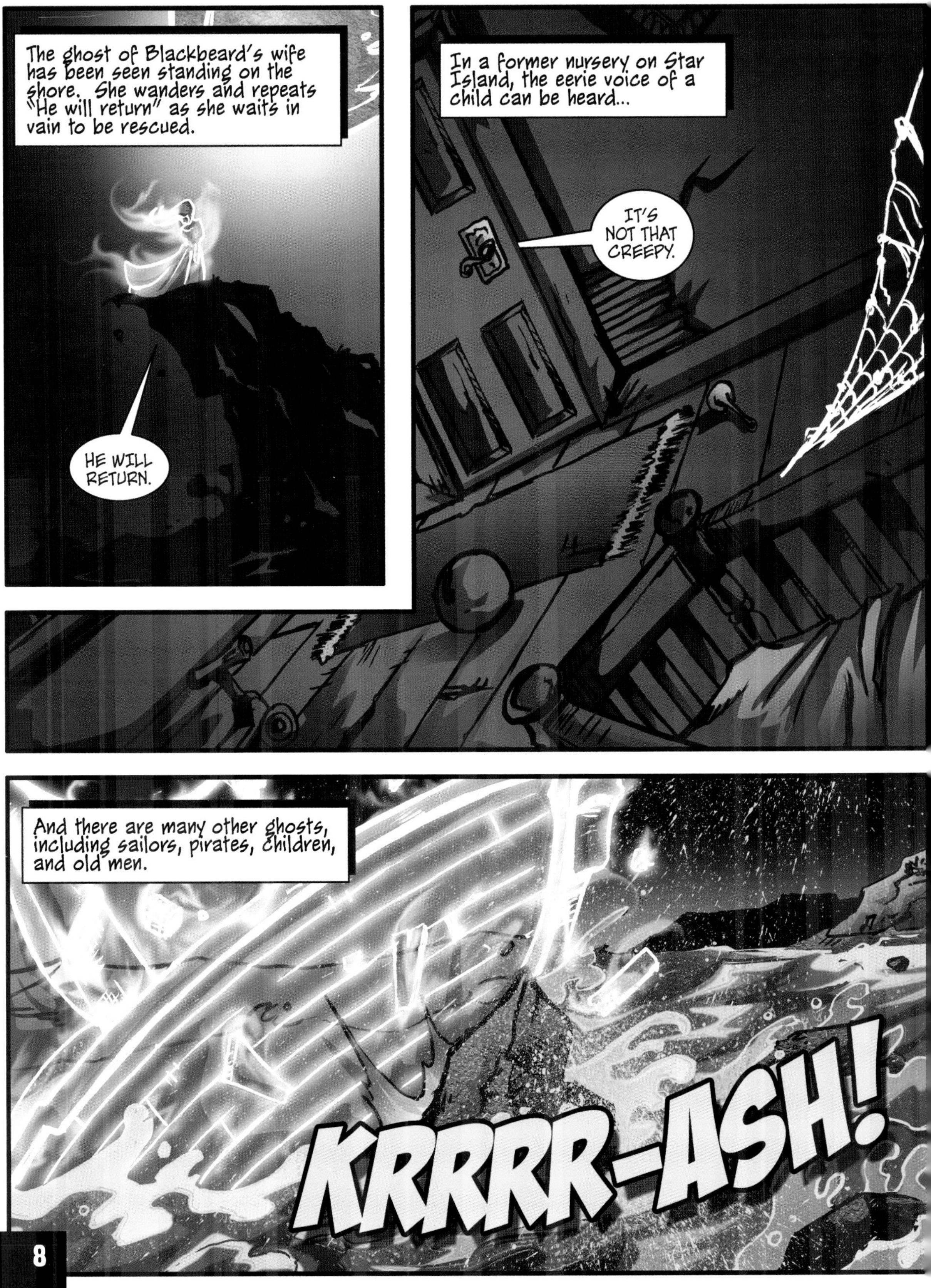

The ghost of Blackbeard's wife has been seen standing on the shore. She wanders and repeats "He will return" as she waits in vain to be rescued.
HE WILL RETURN.
In a former nursery on Star Island, the eerie voice of a child can be heard...
IT'S NOT THAT CREEPY.
And there are many other ghosts, including sailors, pirates, children, and old men.
KRRRR-ASH!

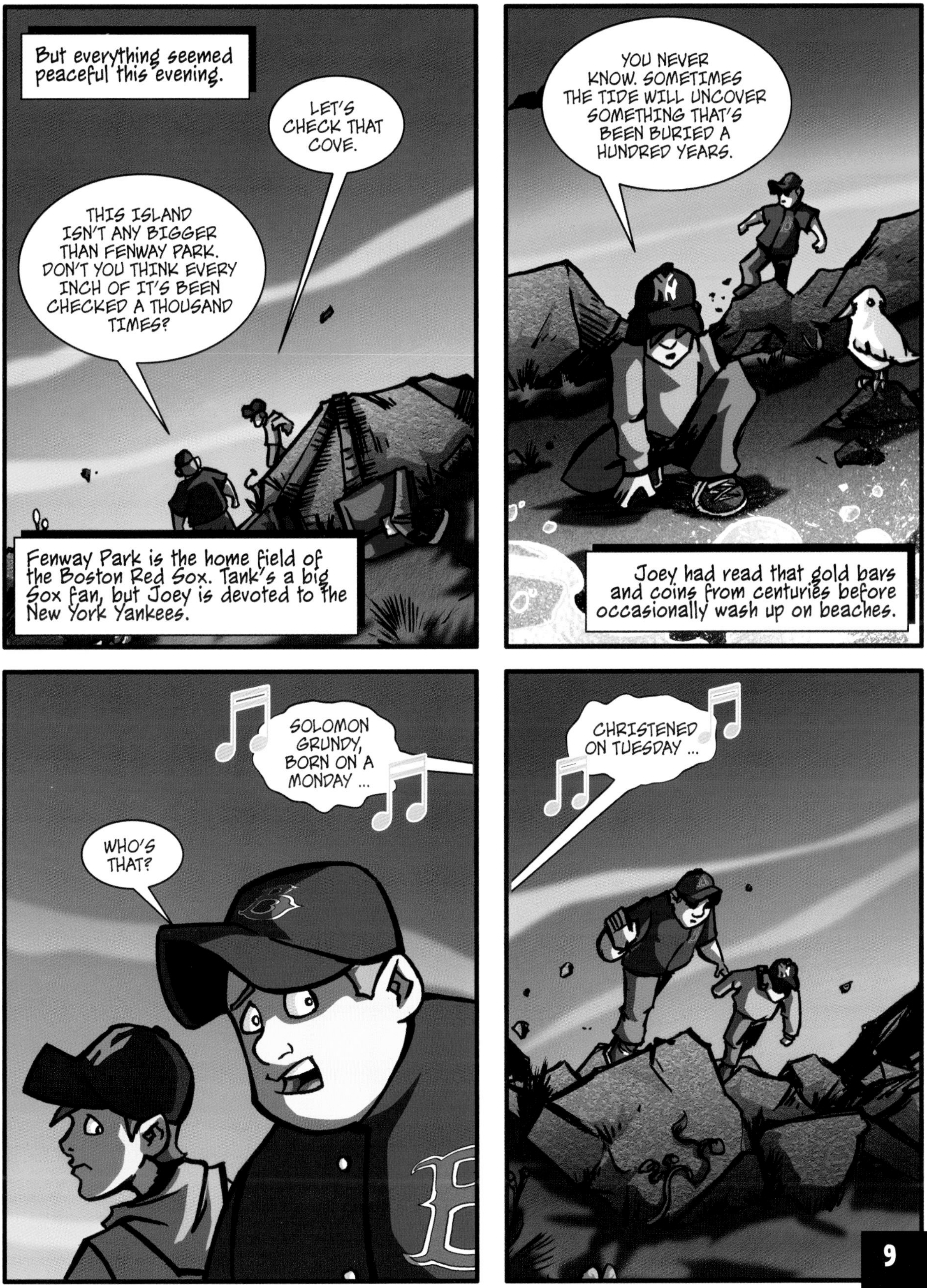
But everything seemed peaceful this evening.
LET'S CHECK THAT COVE.
THIS ISLAND ISN'T ANY BIGGER THAN FENWAY PARK. DON'T YOU THINK EVERY INCH OF IT'S BEEN CHECKED A THOUSAND TIMES?
Fenway Park is the home field of the Boston Red Sox. Tank's a big Sox fan, but Joey is devoted to the New York Yankees.
YOU NEVER KNOW. SOMETIMES THE TIDE WILL UNCOVER SOMETHING THAT'S BEEN BURIED A HUNDRED YEARS.
Joey had read that gold bars and coins from centuries before occasionally wash up on beaches.
SOLOMON GRUNDY, BORN ON A MONDAY ...
WHO'S THAT?
CHRISTENED ON TUESDAY ...

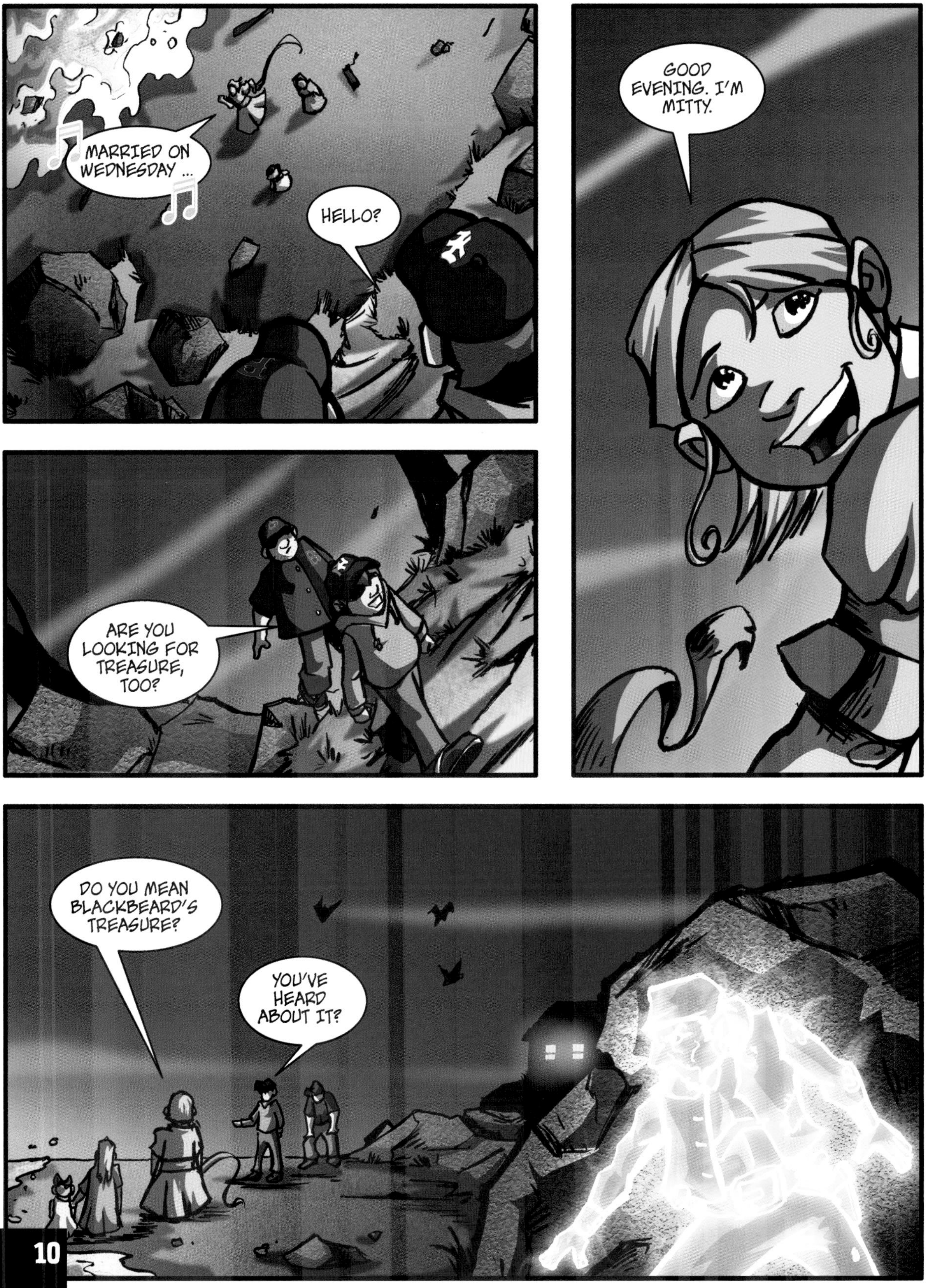
MARRIED ON WEDNESDAY ...
HELLO?
GOOD EVENING. I'M MITTY.
ARE YOU LOOKING FOR TREASURE, TOO?
DO YOU MEAN BLACKBEARD'S TREASURE?
YOU'VE HEARD ABOUT IT?

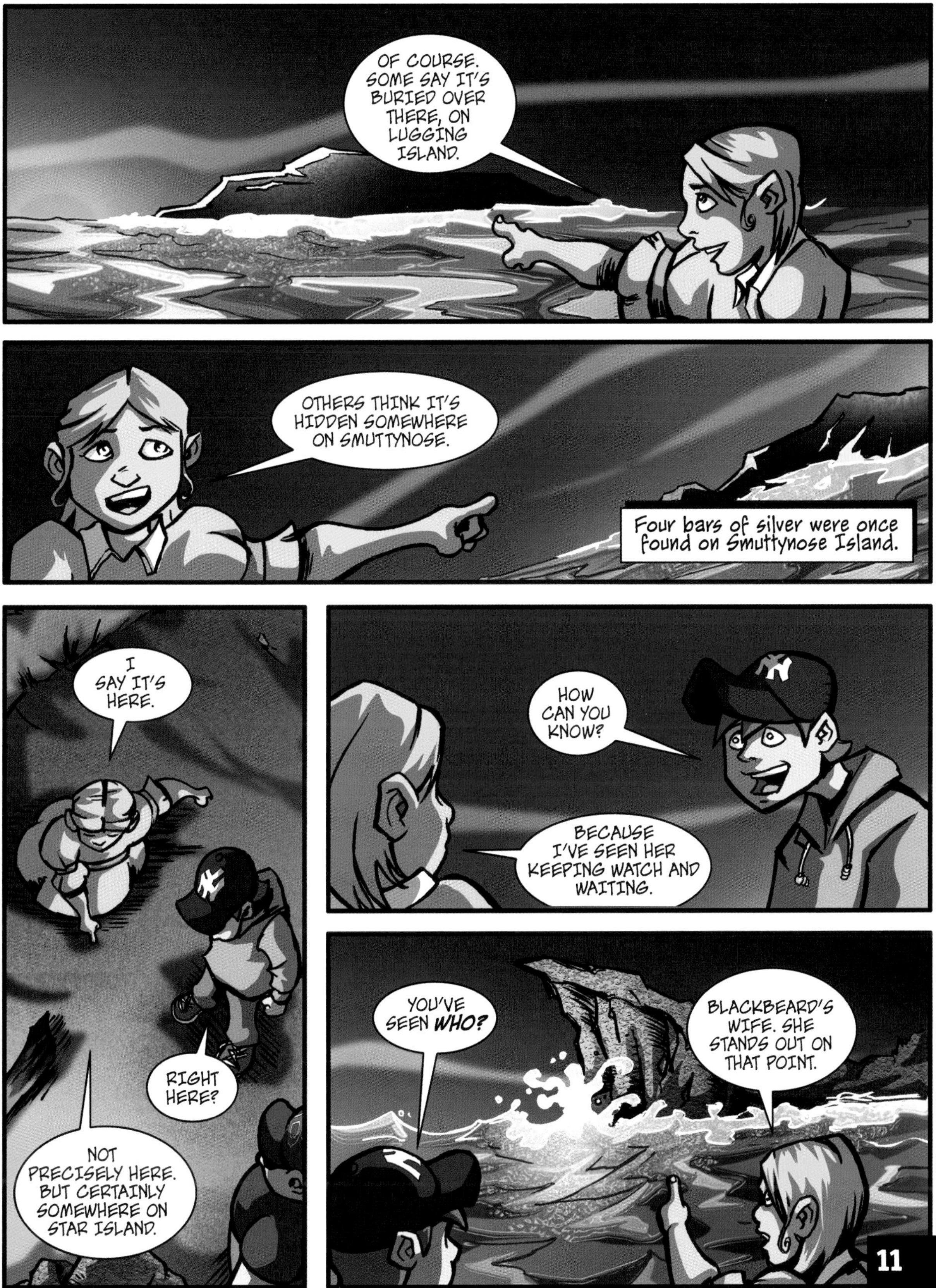

OF COURSE. SOME SAY IT'S BURIED OVER THERE, ON LUGGING ISLAND.
OTHERS THINK IT'S HIDDEN SOMEWHERE ON SMUTTYNOSE.
Four bars of silver were once found on Smuttynose Island.
I SAY IT'S HERE.
RIGHT HERE?
NOT PRECISELY HERE. BUT CERTAINLY SOMEWHERE ON STAR ISLAND.
HOW CAN YOU KNOW?
BECAUSE I'VE SEEN HER KEEPING WATCH AND WAITING.
YOU'VE SEEN WHO?
BLACKBEARD'S WIFE. SHE STANDS OUT ON THAT POINT.

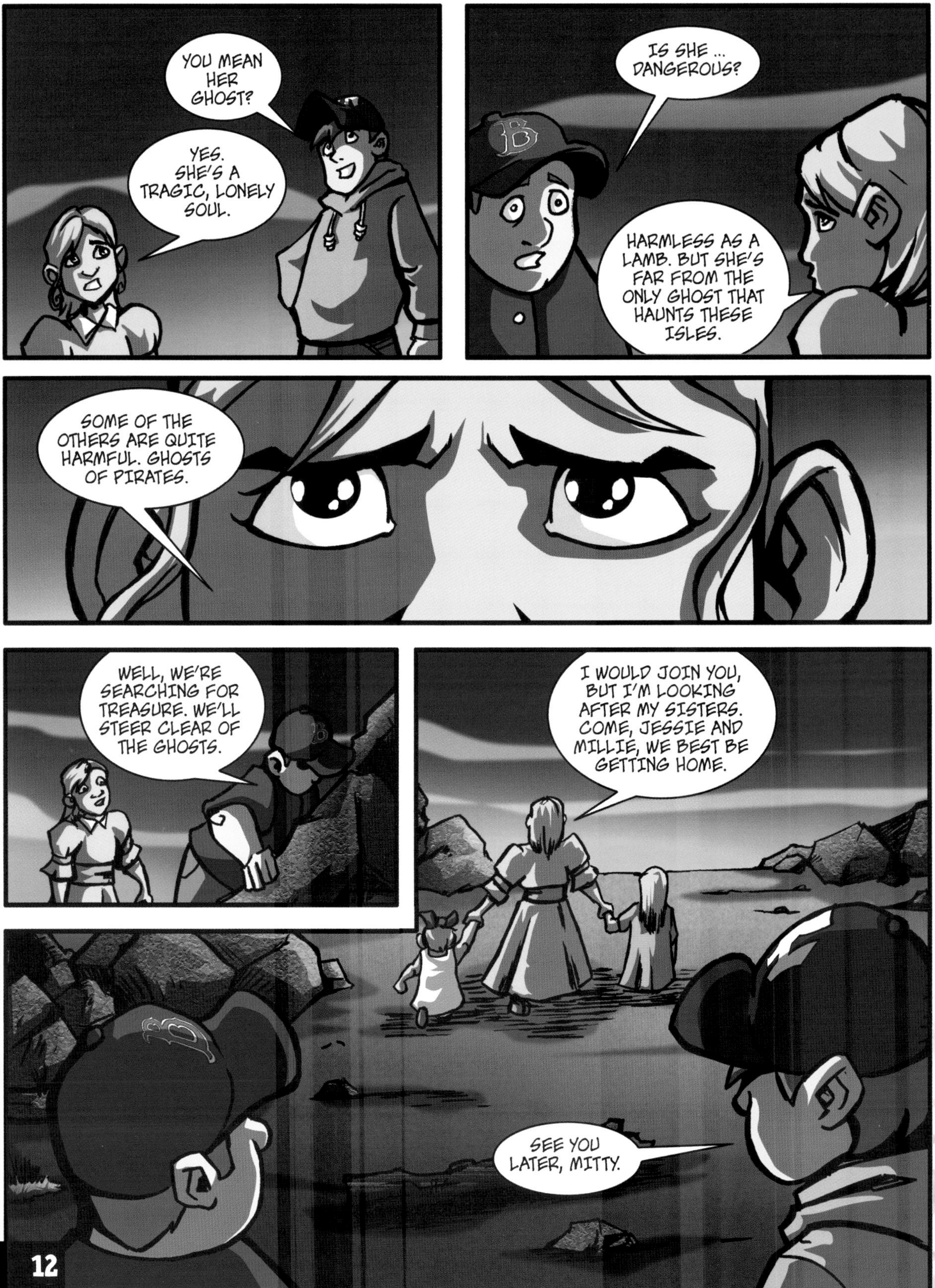
YOU MEAN HER GHOST?
YES. SHE'S A TRAGIC, LONELY SOUL.
IS SHE ... DANGEROUS?
HARMLESS AS A LAMB. BUT SHE'S FAR FROM THE ONLY GHOST THAT HAUNTS THESE ISLES.
SOME OF THE OTHERS ARE QUITE HARMFUL. GHOSTS OF PIRATES.
WELL, WE'RE SEARCHING FOR TREASURE. WE'LL STEER CLEAR OF THE GHOSTS.
I WOULD JOIN YOU, BUT I'M LOOKING AFTER MY SISTERS. COME, JESSIE AND MILLIE, WE BEST BE GETTING HOME.
SEE YOU LATER, MITTY.

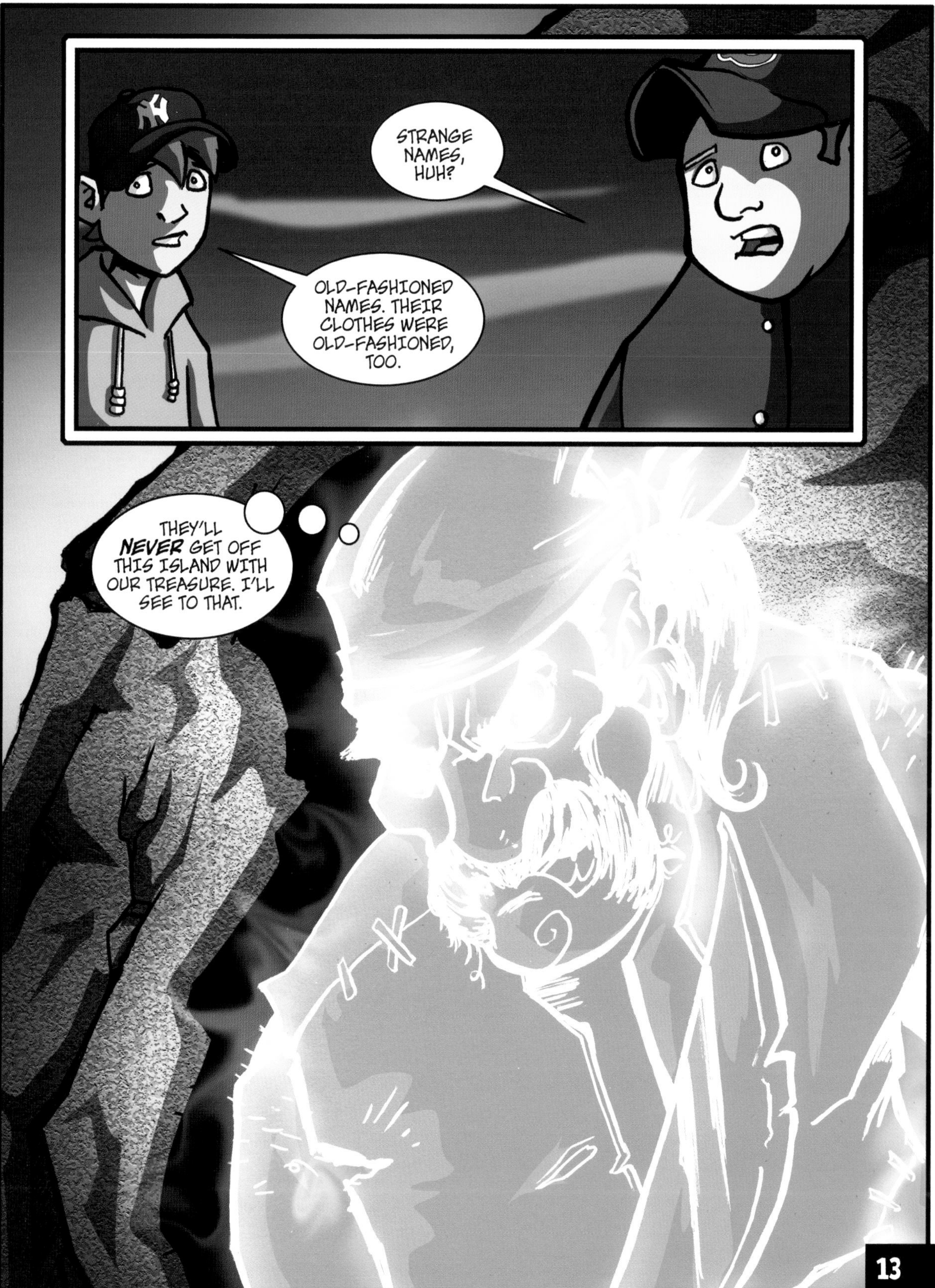
STRANGE NAMES, HUH?
OLD-FASHIONED NAMES. THEIR CLOTHES WERE OLD-FASHIONED, TOO.
THEY'LL NEVER GET OFF THIS ISLAND WITH OUR TREASURE. I'LL SEE TO THAT.

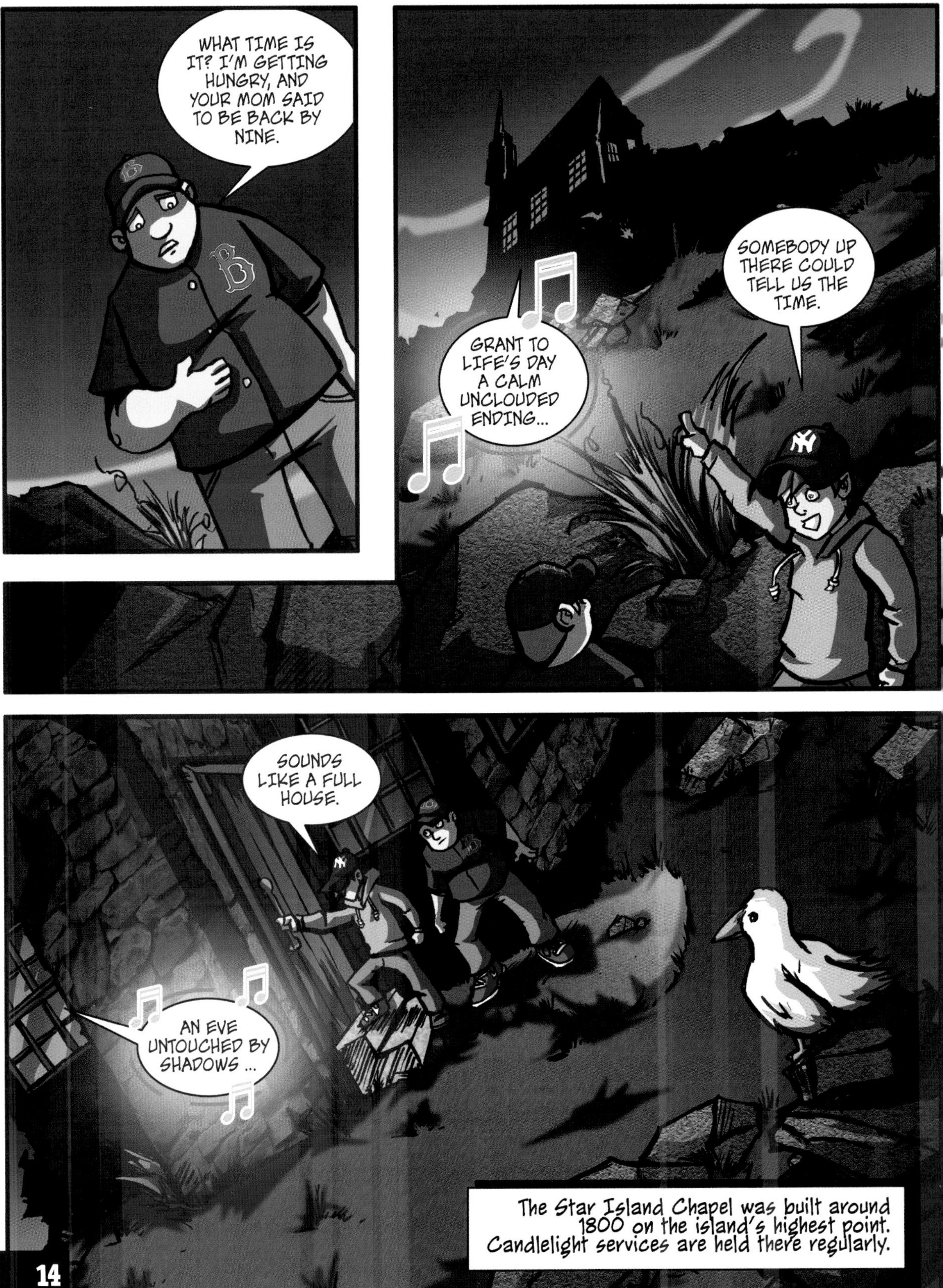
WHAT TIME IS IT? I'M GETTING HUNGRY, AND YOUR MOM SAID TO BE BACK BY NINE.
SOMEBODY UP THERE COULD TELL US THE TIME.
GRANT TO LIFE'S DAY A CALM UNCLOUDED ENDING...
SOUNDS LIKE A FULL HOUSE.
AN EVE UNTOUCHED BY SHADOWS ...
The Star Island Chapel was built around 1800 on the island's highest point. Candlelight services are held there regularly.

The chapel was empty and silent.

HUH?

WHERE'D EVERYBODY GO?

CREEEEAK-ECK

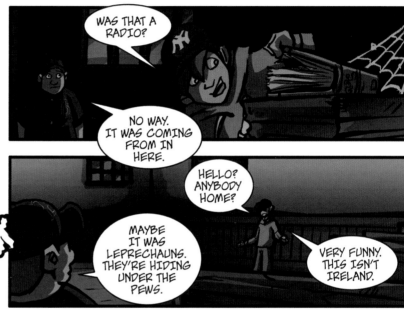

WAS THAT A RADIO?

NO WAY. IT WAS COMING FROM IN HERE.

HELLO? ANYBODY HOME?

MAYBE IT WAS LEPRECHAUNS. THEY'RE HIDING UNDER THE PEWS.

VERY FUNNY. THIS ISN'T IRELAND.

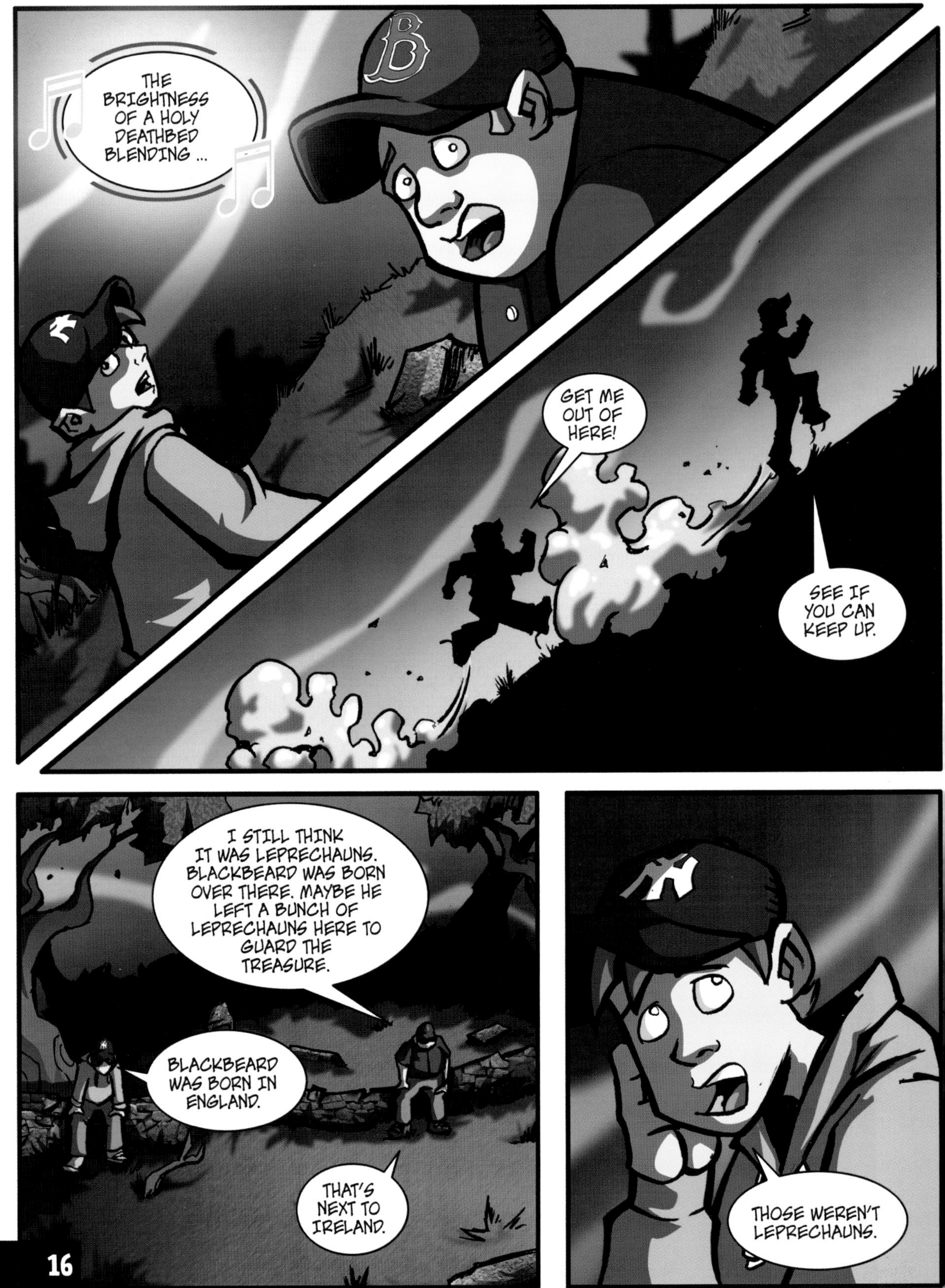

THE BRIGHTNESS OF A HOLY DEATHBED BLENDING ...
GET ME OUT OF HERE!
SEE IF YOU CAN KEEP UP.
I STILL THINK IT WAS LEPRECHAUNS. BLACKBEARD WAS BORN OVER THERE. MAYBE HE LEFT A BUNCH OF LEPRECHAUNS HERE TO GUARD THE TREASURE.
BLACKBEARD WAS BORN IN ENGLAND.
THAT'S NEXT TO IRELAND.
THOSE WEREN'T LEPRECHAUNS.

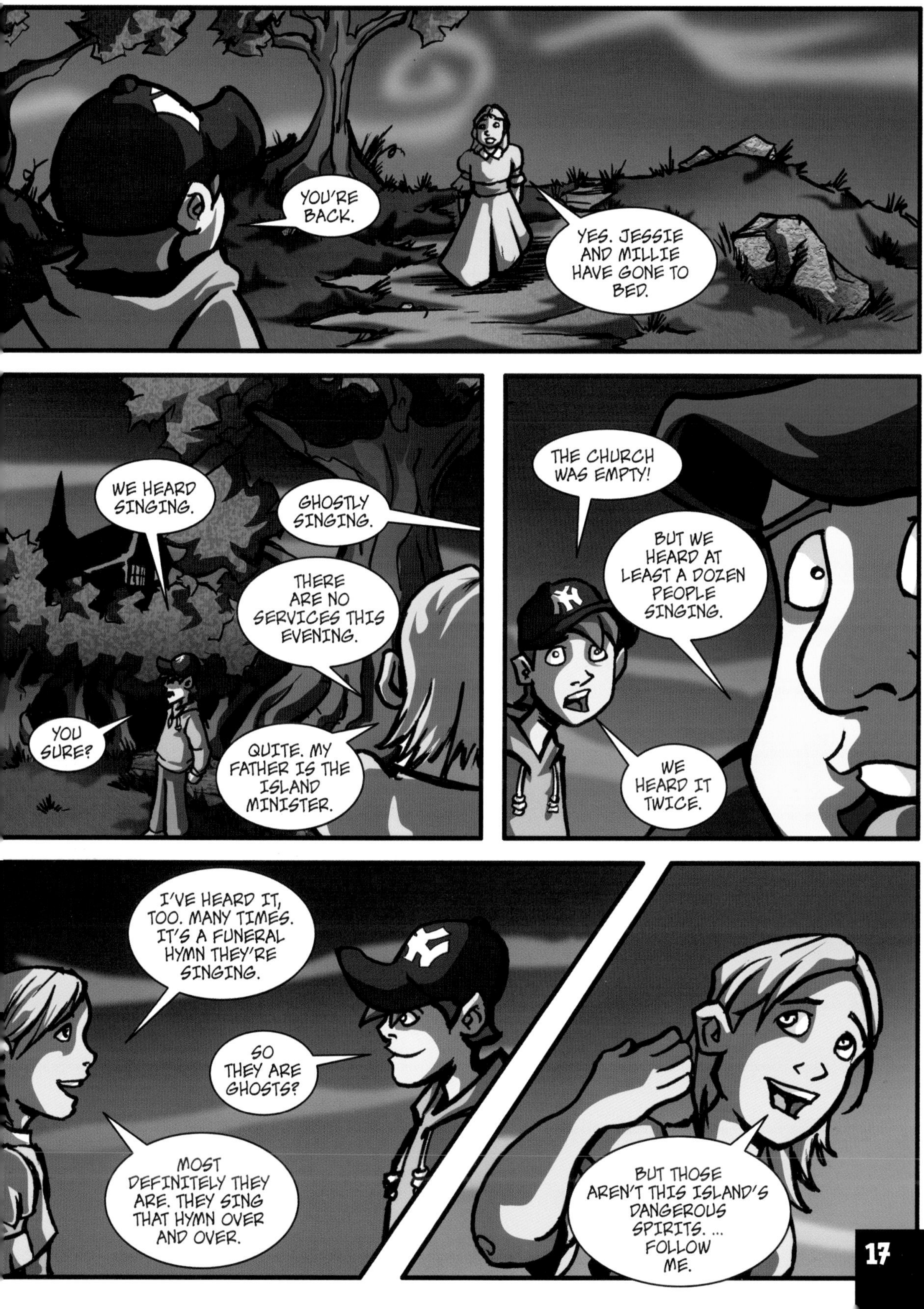
YOU'RE BACK.
YES. JESSIE AND MILLIE HAVE GONE TO BED.
WE HEARD SINGING.
GHOSTLY SINGING.
THERE ARE NO SERVICES THIS EVENING.
YOU SURE?
QUITE. MY FATHER IS THE ISLAND MINISTER.
THE CHURCH WAS EMPTY!
BUT WE HEARD AT LEAST A DOZEN PEOPLE SINGING.
WE HEARD IT TWICE.
I'VE HEARD IT, TOO. MANY TIMES. IT'S A FUNERAL HYMN THEY'RE SINGING.
SO THEY ARE GHOSTS?
MOST DEFINITELY THEY ARE. THEY SING THAT HYMN OVER AND OVER.
BUT THOSE AREN'T THIS ISLAND'S DANGEROUS SPIRITS. ... FOLLOW ME.

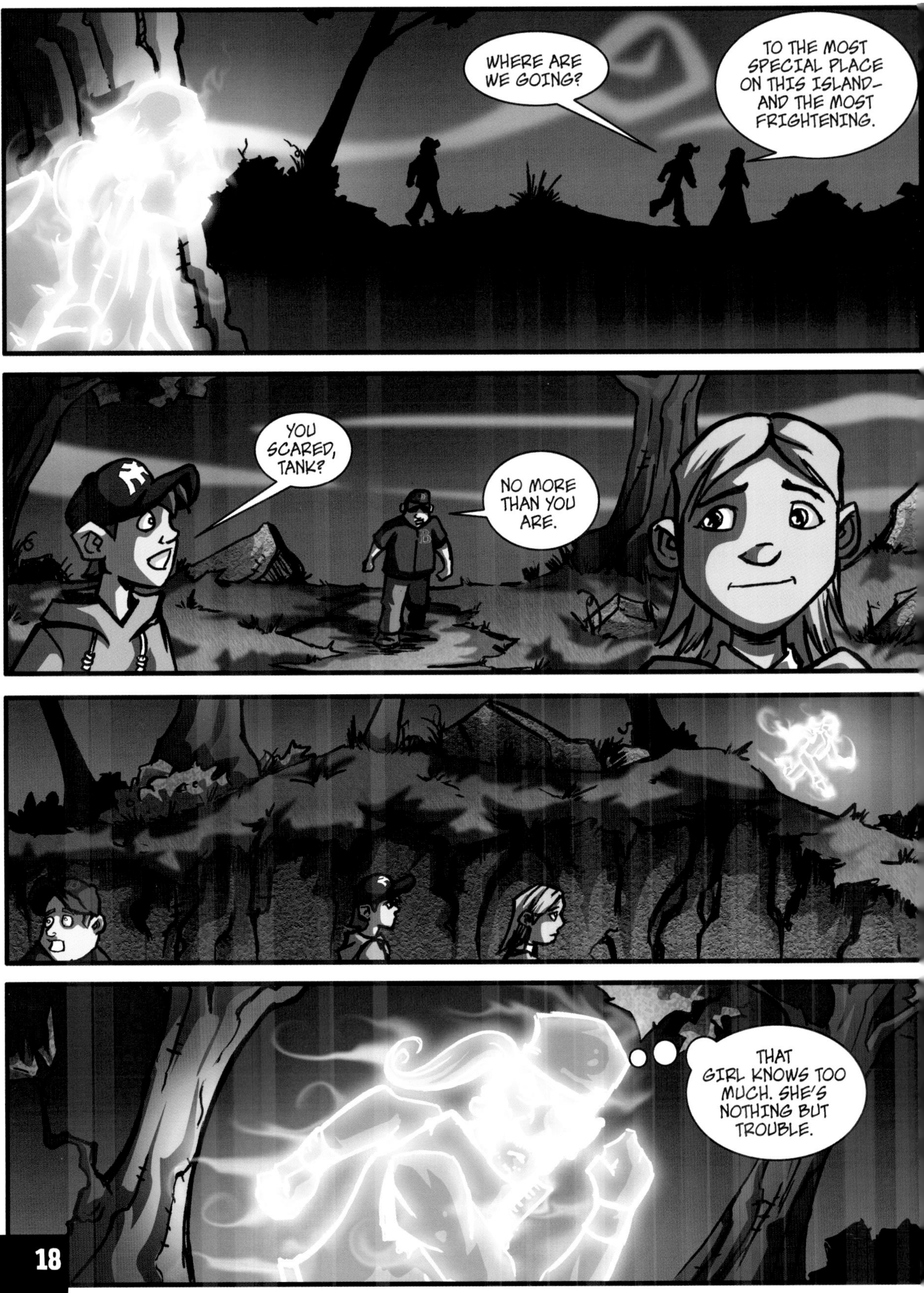
WHERE ARE WE GOING?
TO THE MOST SPECIAL PLACE ON THIS ISLAND– AND THE MOST FRIGHTENING.
YOU SCARED, TANK?
NO MORE THAN YOU ARE.
THAT GIRL KNOWS TOO MUCH. SHE'S NOTHING BUT TROUBLE.

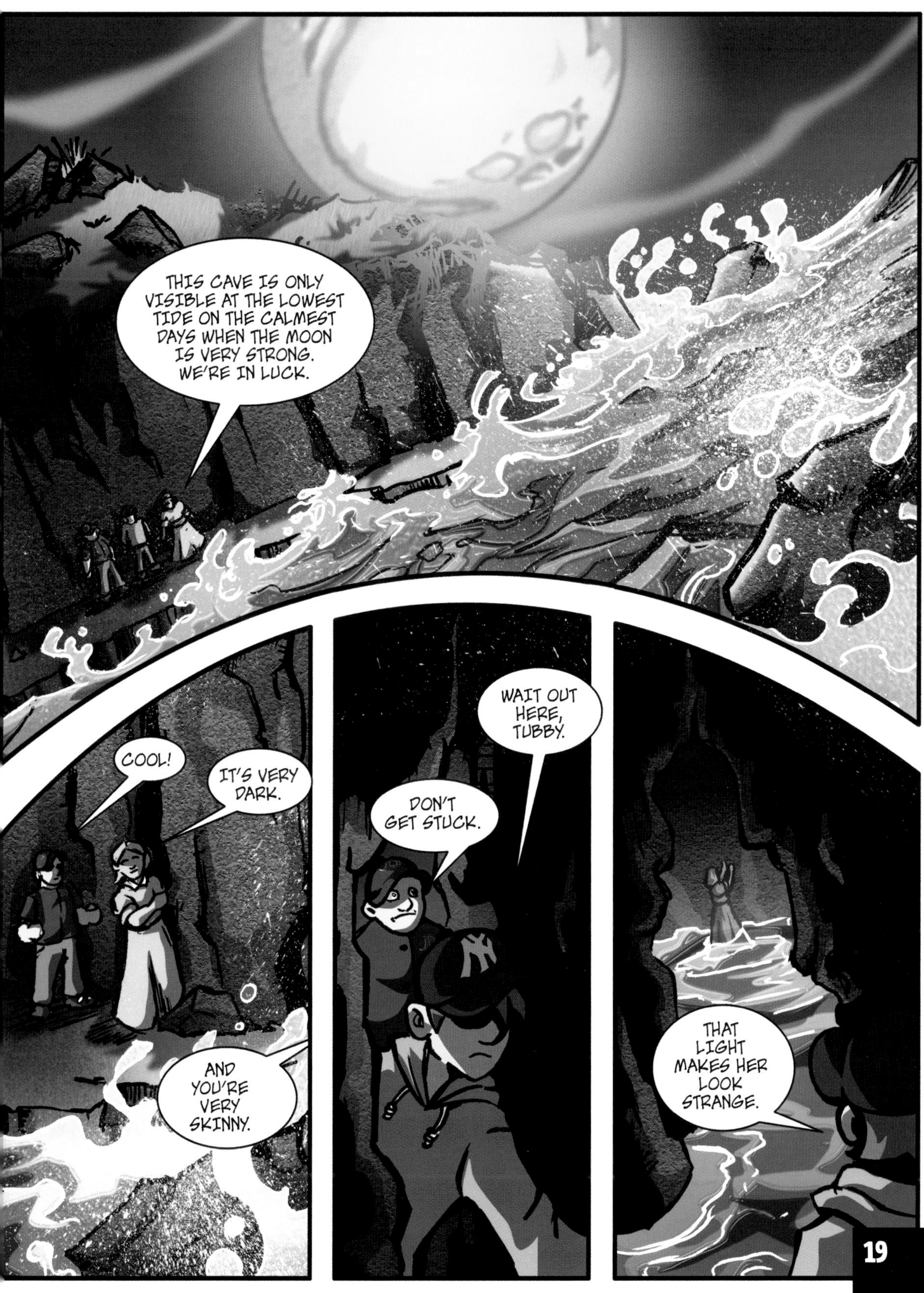
THIS CAVE IS ONLY VISIBLE AT THE LOWEST TIDE ON THE CALMEST DAYS WHEN THE MOON IS VERY STRONG. WE'RE IN LUCK.
COOL!
IT'S VERY DARK.
AND YOU'RE VERY SKINNY.
WAIT OUT HERE, TUBBY.
DON'T GET STUCK.
THAT LIGHT MAKES HER LOOK STRANGE.

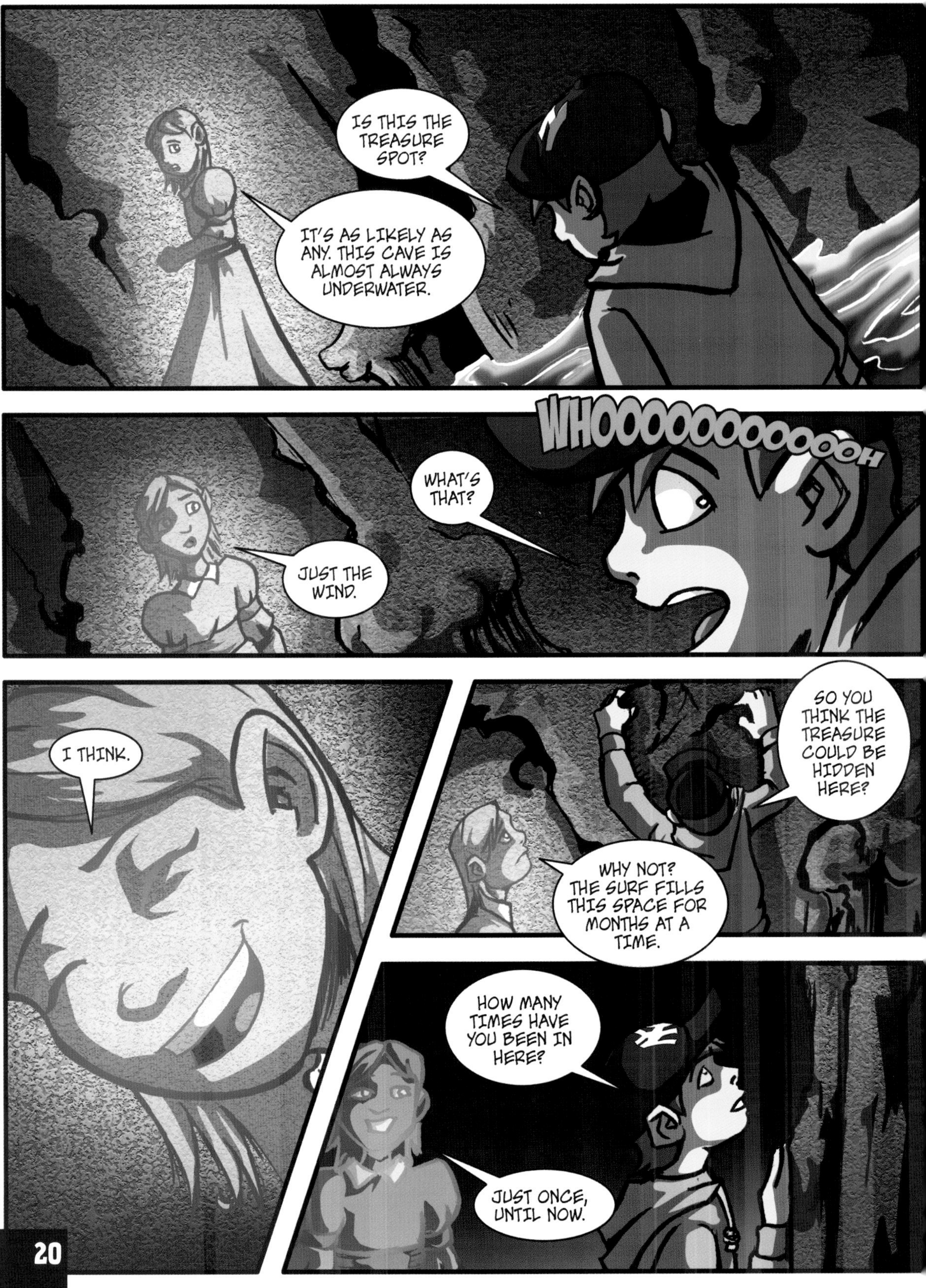
IS THIS THE TREASURE SPOT?
IT'S AS LIKELY AS ANY. THIS CAVE IS ALMOST ALWAYS UNDERWATER.
WHOOOOOOOOOOOOOH
WHAT'S THAT?
JUST THE WIND.
I THINK.
SO YOU THINK THE TREASURE COULD BE HIDDEN HERE?
WHY NOT? THE SURF FILLS THIS SPACE FOR MONTHS AT A TIME.
HOW MANY TIMES HAVE YOU BEEN IN HERE?
JUST ONCE, UNTIL NOW.

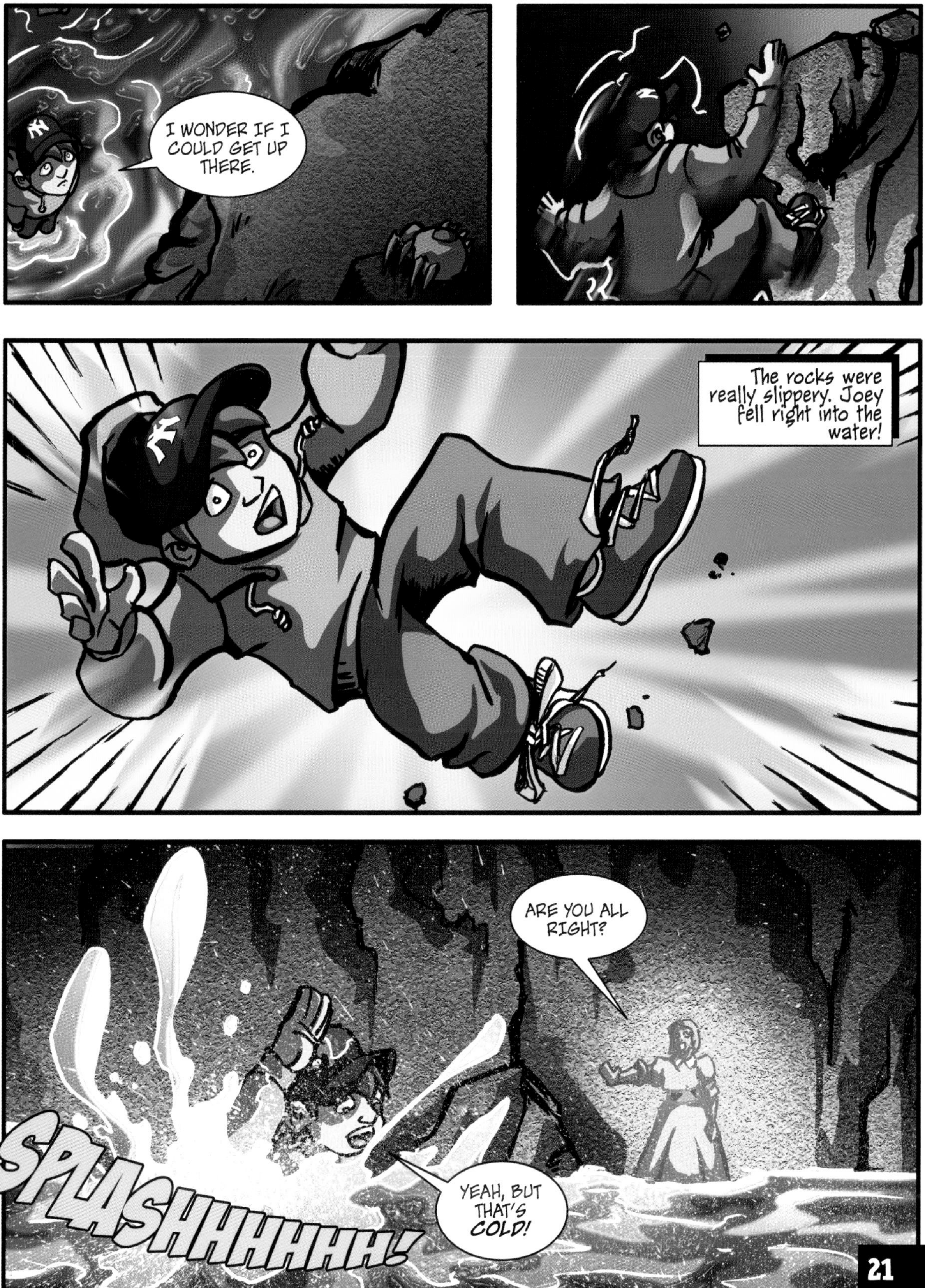
I WONDER IF I COULD GET UP THERE.
The rocks were really slippery. Joey fell right into the water!
ARE YOU ALL RIGHT?
SPLASHHHHHHH!
YEAH, BUT THAT'S COLD!

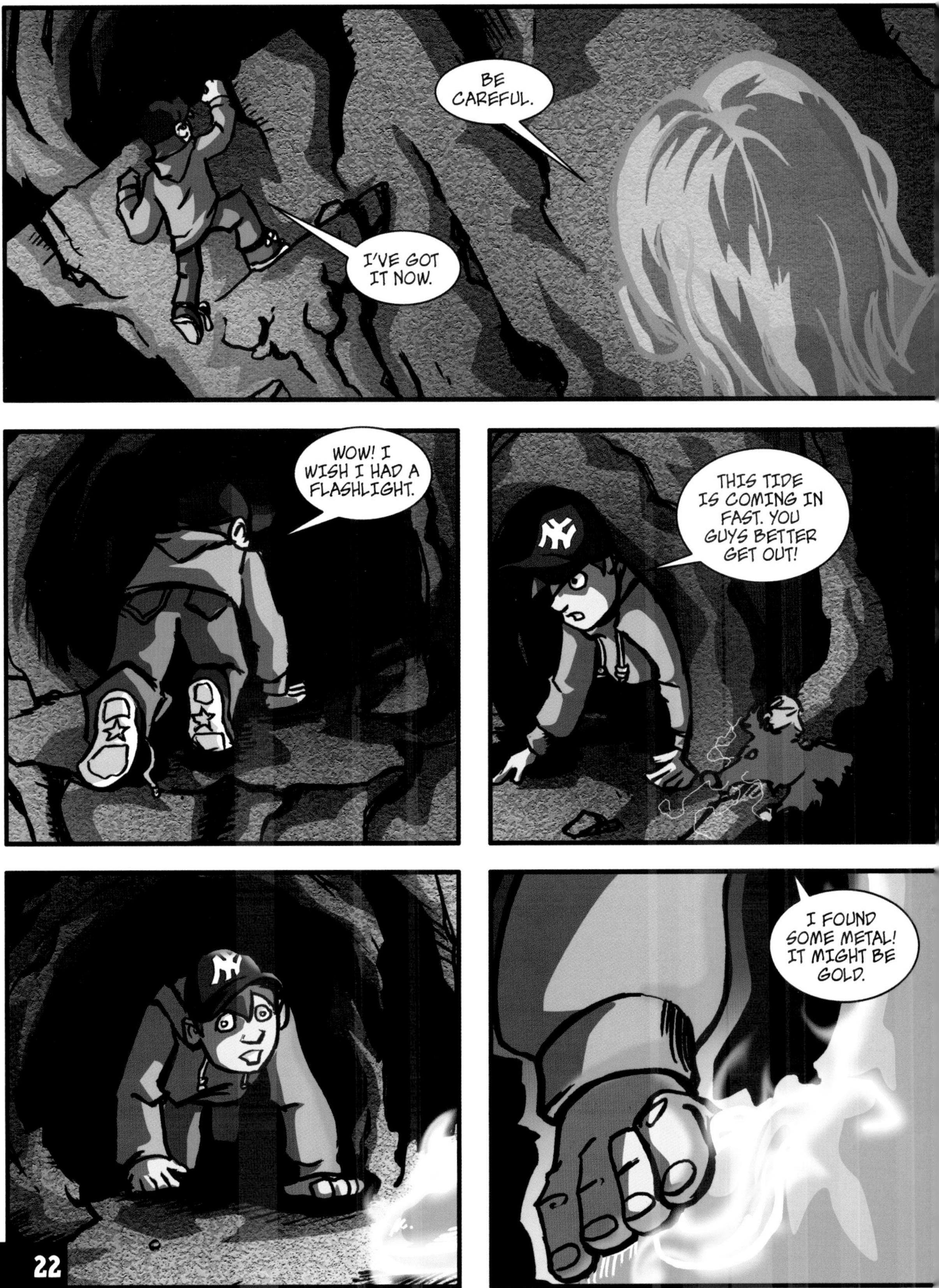
BE CAREFUL.
I'VE GOT IT NOW.
WOW! I WISH I HAD A FLASHLIGHT.
THIS TIDE IS COMING IN FAST. YOU GUYS BETTER GET OUT!
I FOUND SOME METAL! IT MIGHT BE GOLD.

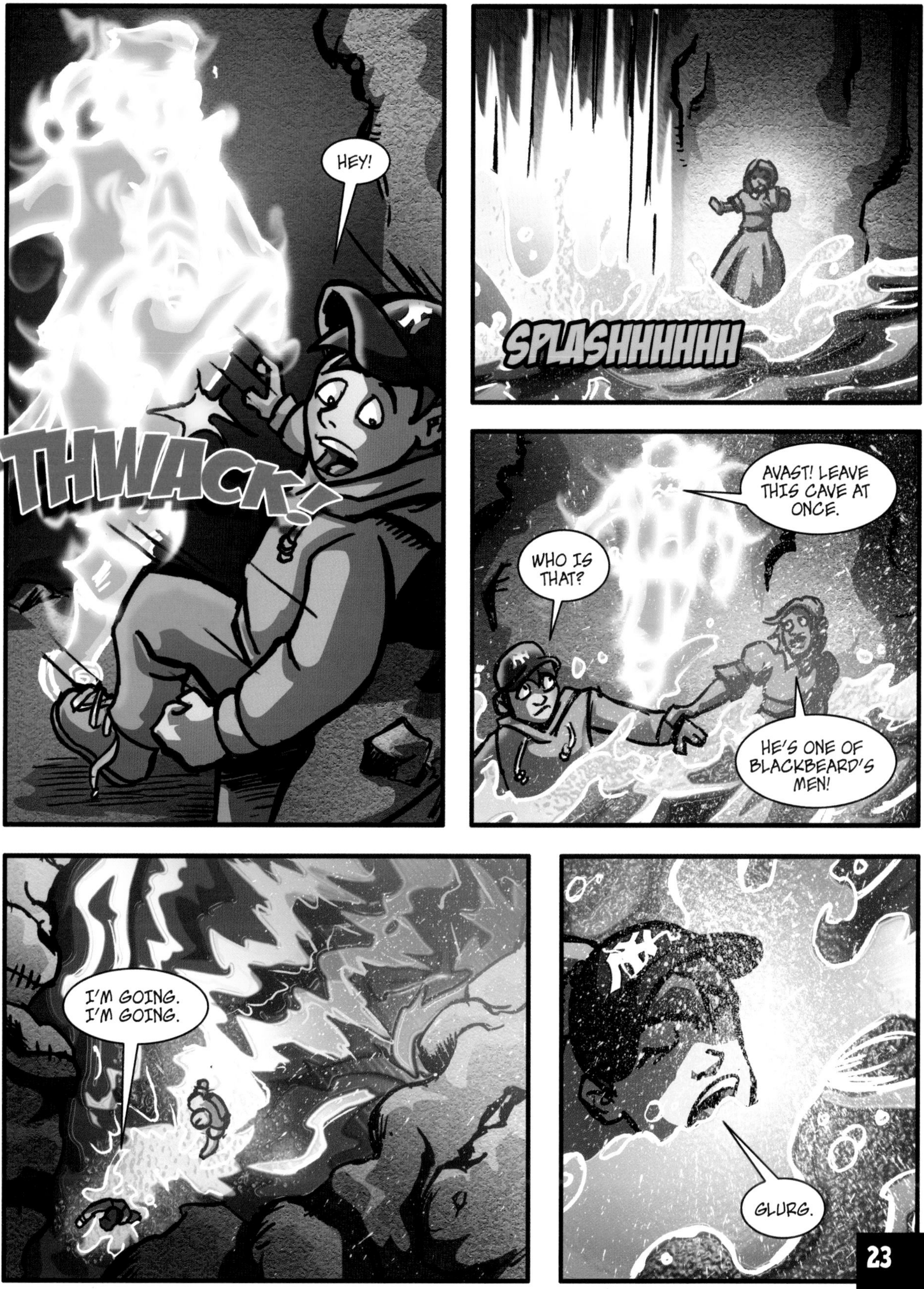
HEY!
THWACK!
SPLASHHHHHH
AVAST! LEAVE THIS CAVE AT ONCE.
WHO IS THAT?
HE'S ONE OF BLACKBEARD'S MEN!
I'M GOING. I'M GOING.
GLURG.

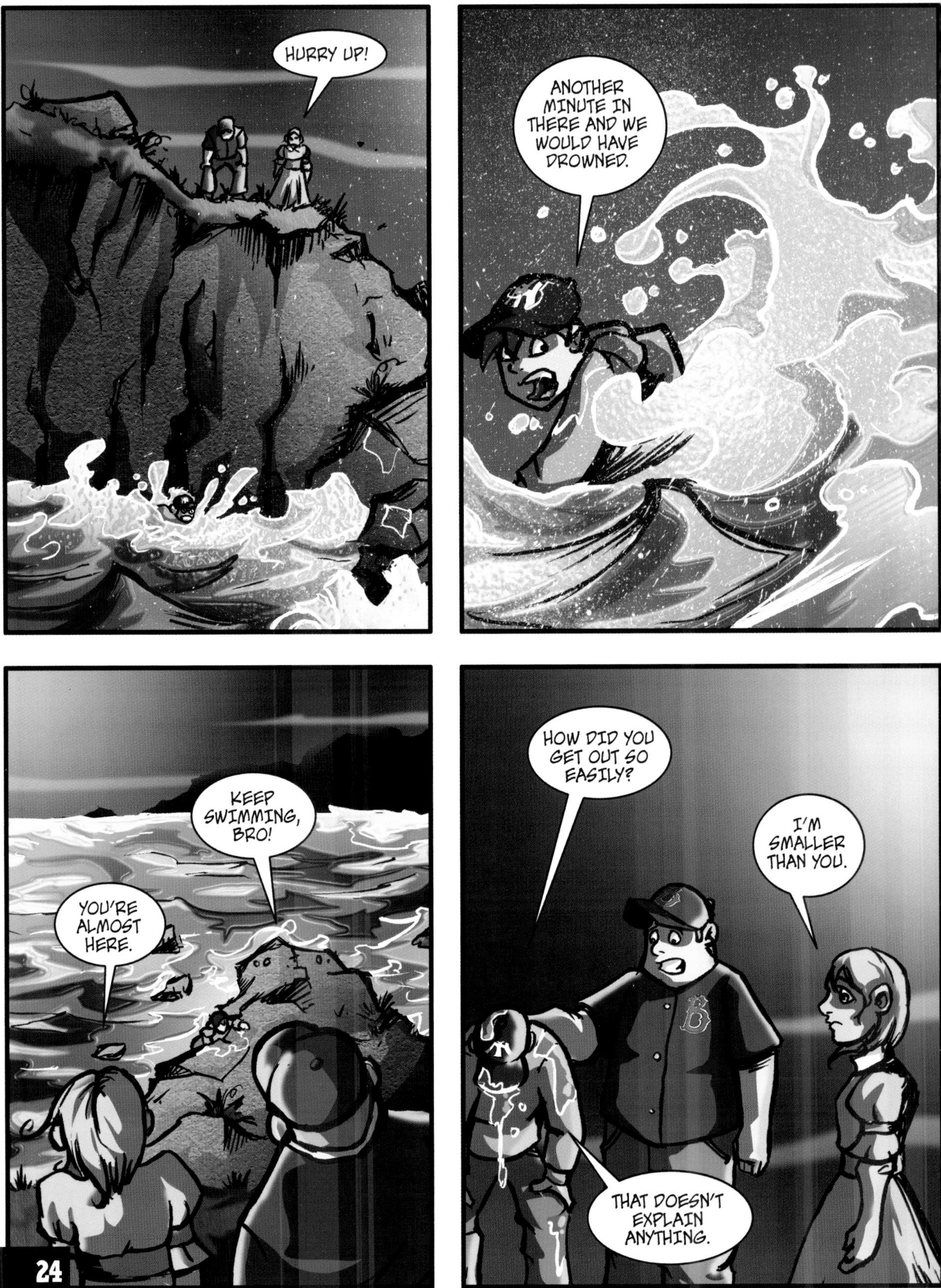
HURRY UP!
ANOTHER MINUTE IN THERE AND WE WOULD HAVE DROWNED.
KEEP SWIMMING, BRO!
YOU'RE ALMOST HERE.
HOW DID YOU GET OUT SO EASILY?
I'M SMALLER THAN YOU.
THAT DOESN'T EXPLAIN ANYTHING.

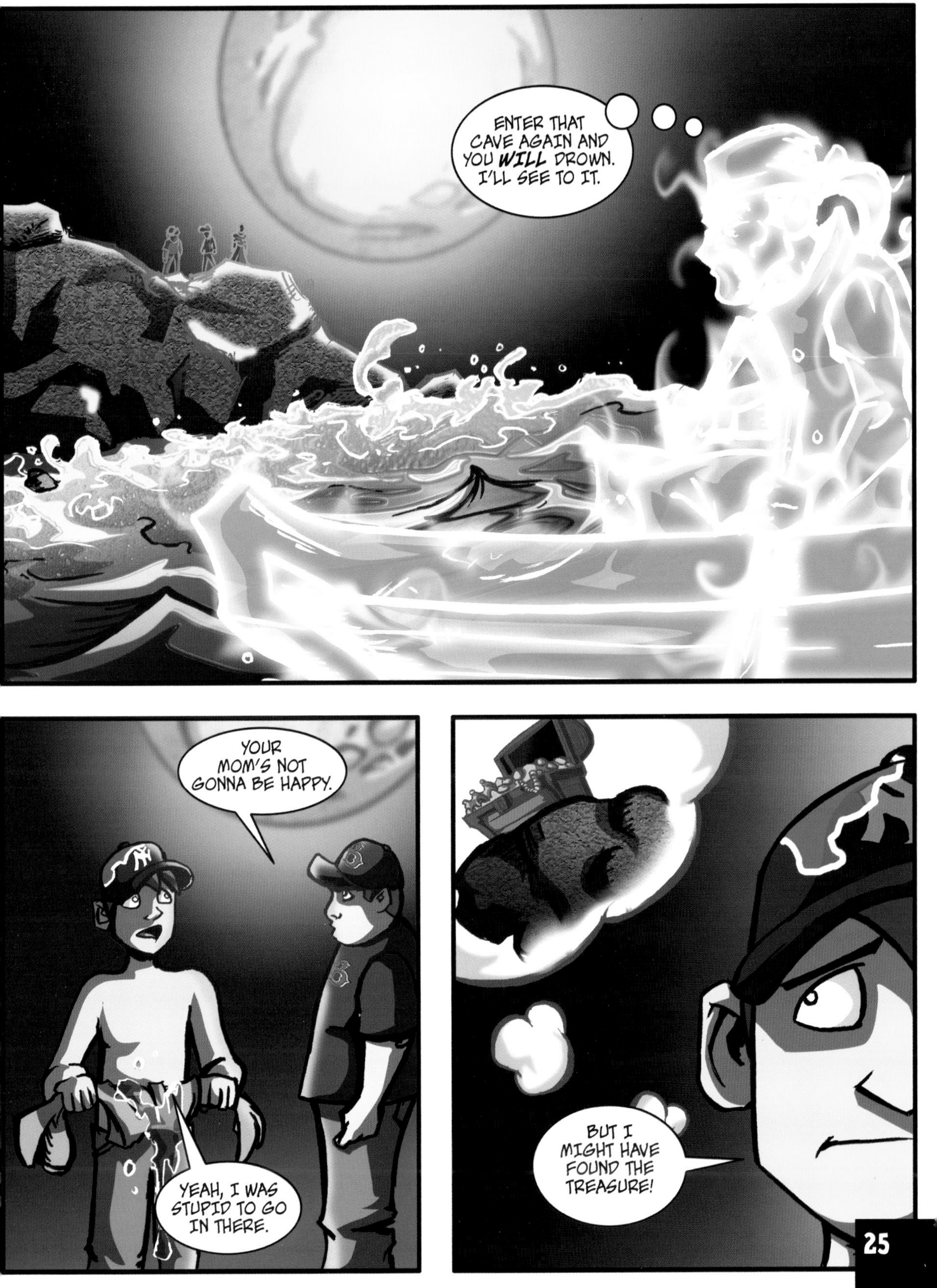
ENTER THAT CAVE AGAIN AND YOU WILL DROWN. I'LL SEE TO IT.
YOUR MOM'S NOT GONNA BE HAPPY.
YEAH, I WAS STUPID TO GO IN THERE.
BUT I MIGHT HAVE FOUND THE TREASURE!

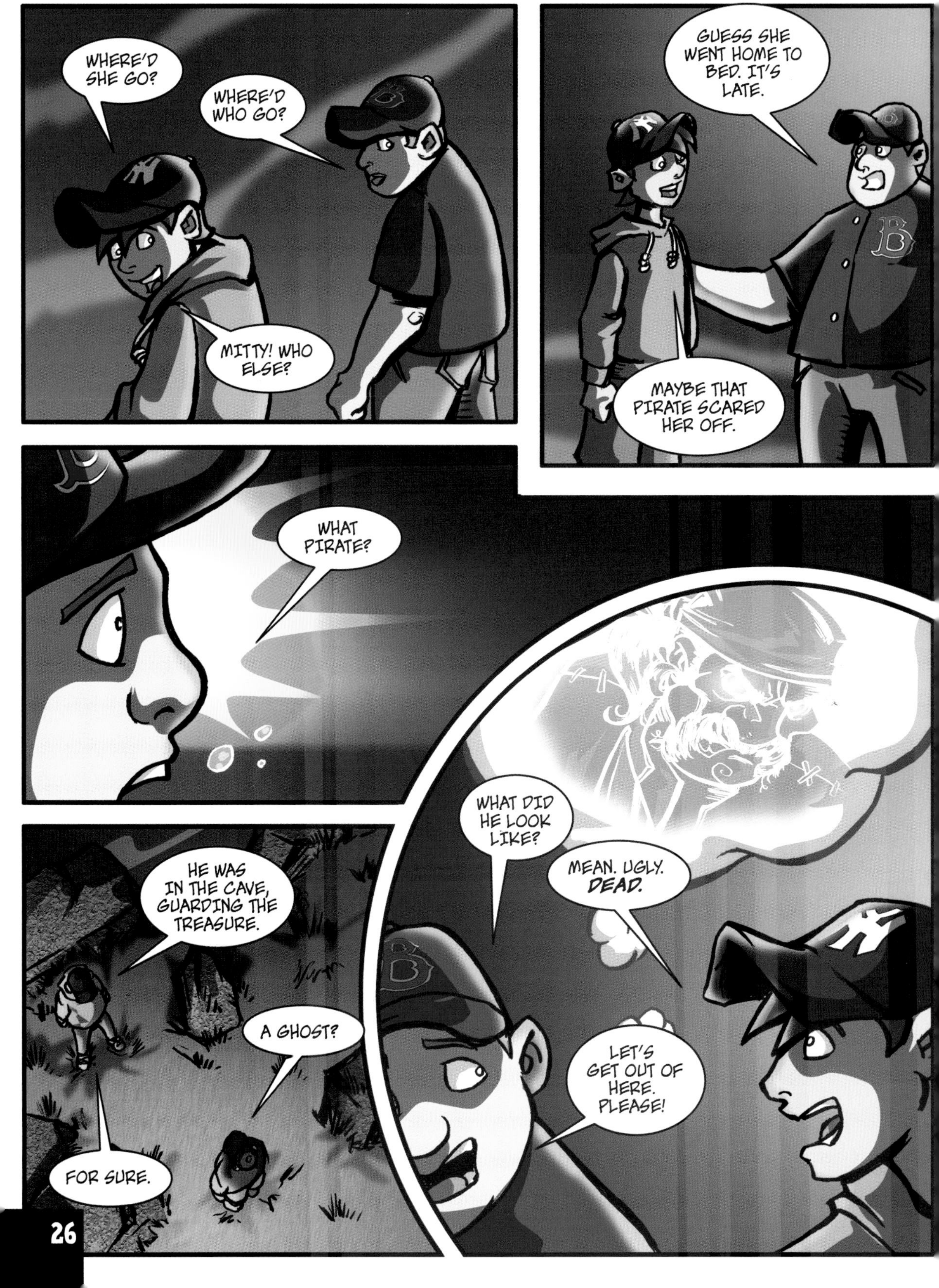
WHERE'D SHE GO?
WHERE'D WHO GO?
MITTY! WHO ELSE?
GUESS SHE WENT HOME TO BED. IT'S LATE.
MAYBE THAT PIRATE SCARED HER OFF.
WHAT PIRATE?
WHAT DID HE LOOK LIKE?
MEAN. UGLY. ***DEAD.***
LET'S GET OUT OF HERE. PLEASE!
HE WAS IN THE CAVE, GUARDING THE TREASURE.
A GHOST?
FOR SURE.

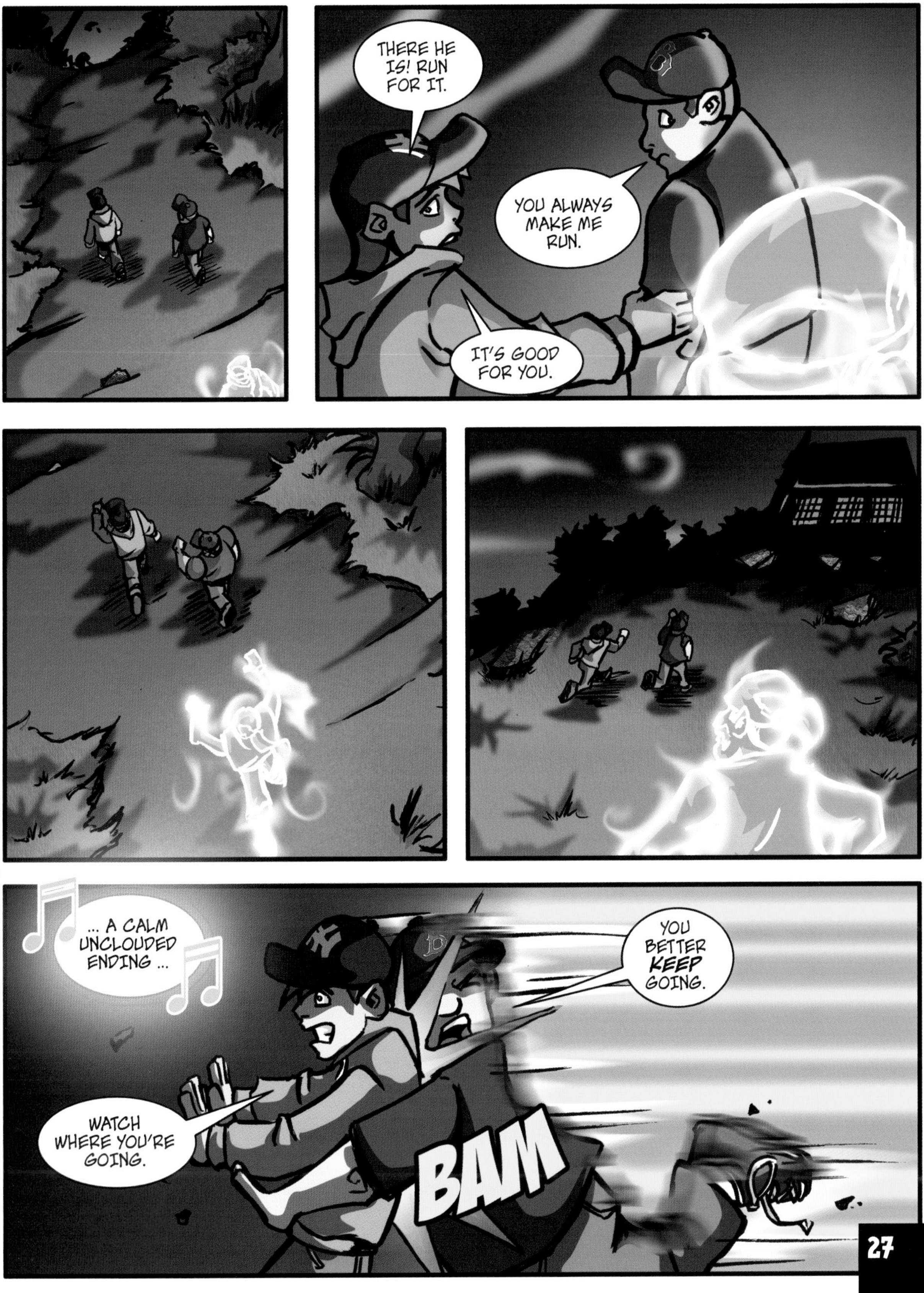
THERE HE IS! RUN FOR IT.
YOU ALWAYS MAKE ME RUN.
IT'S GOOD FOR YOU.
... A CALM UNCLOUDED ENDING ...
YOU BETTER KEEP GOING.
WATCH WHERE YOU'RE GOING.
BAM

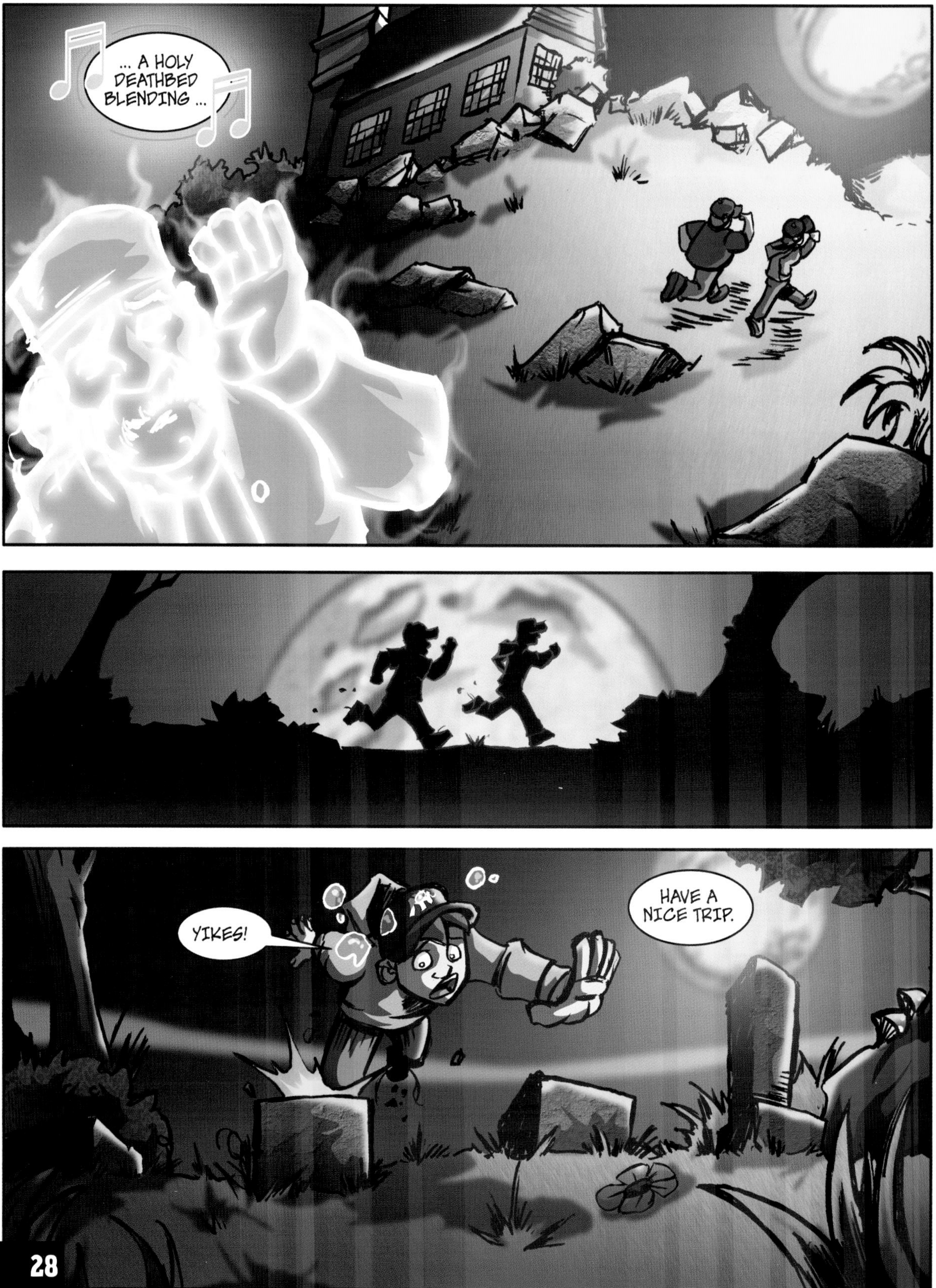
... A HOLY DEATHBED BLENDING ...
YIKES!
HAVE A NICE TRIP.

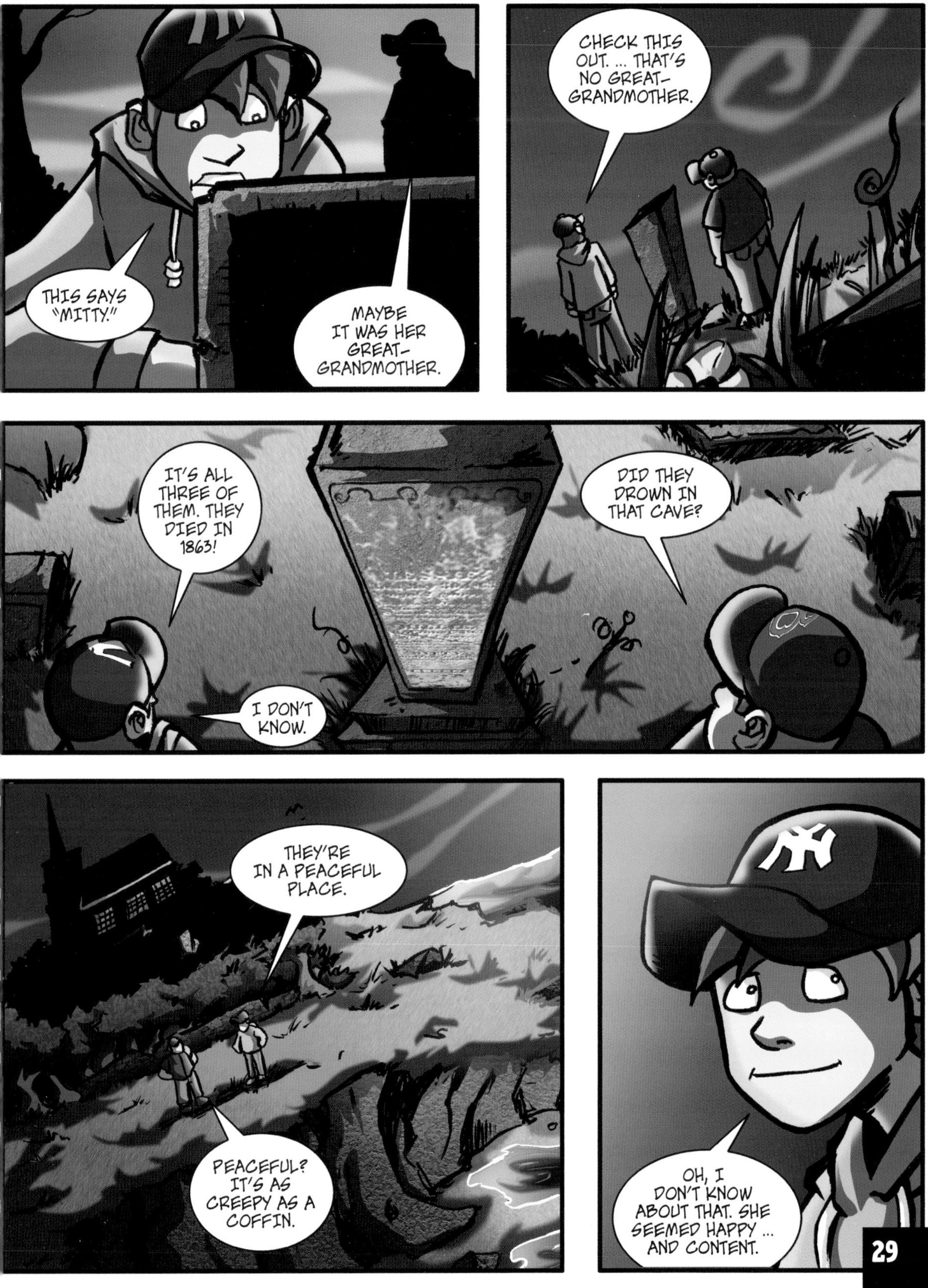
THIS SAYS "MITTY."
MAYBE IT WAS HER GREAT-GRANDMOTHER.
CHECK THIS OUT. ... THAT'S NO GREAT-GRANDMOTHER.
IT'S ALL THREE OF THEM. THEY DIED IN 1863!
DID THEY DROWN IN THAT CAVE?
I DON'T KNOW.
THEY'RE IN A PEACEFUL PLACE.
PEACEFUL? IT'S AS CREEPY AS A COFFIN.
OH, I DON'T KNOW ABOUT THAT. SHE SEEMED HAPPY ... AND CONTENT.

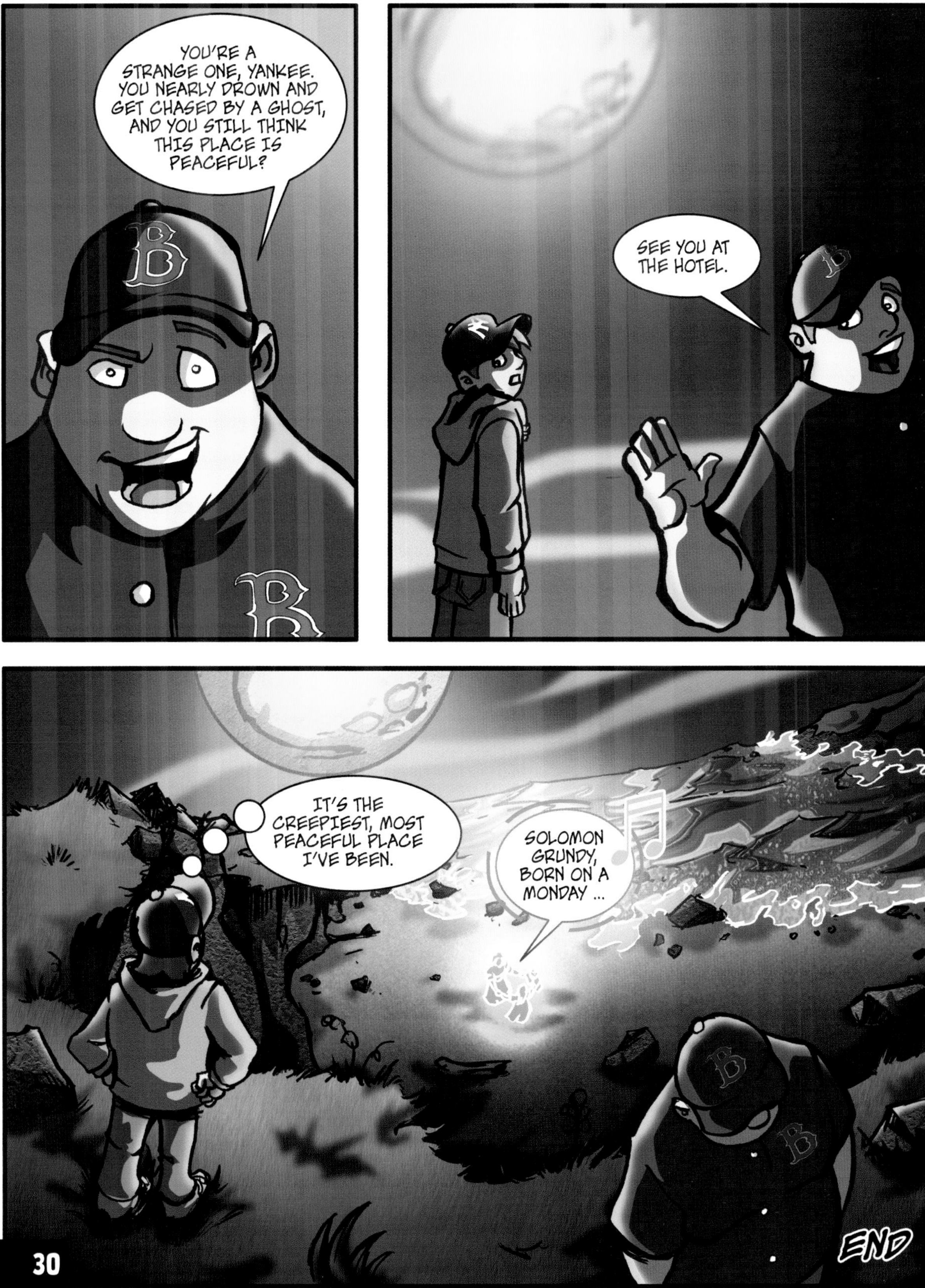
YOU'RE A STRANGE ONE, YANKEE. YOU NEARLY DROWN AND GET CHASED BY A GHOST, AND YOU STILL THINK THIS PLACE IS PEACEFUL?
SEE YOU AT THE HOTEL.
IT'S THE CREEPIEST, MOST PEACEFUL PLACE I'VE BEEN.
SOLOMON GRUNDY, BORN ON A MONDAY ...
END

# STAR ISLAND

Star is the second largest of the nine islands in the Isles of Shoals. The Isles of Shoals lie in the Gulf of Maine near Portsmouth, New Hampshire. Five of the islands are in Maine and four are in New Hampshire. All nine islands are quite small.

The pirate Blackbeard spent time in the Isles of Shoals. It's said that he left treasure on more than one of the islands. People have reported seeing his ghost and the ghost of his wife. His wife was left on one of the islands to guard the treasure, but Blackbeard never returned for her.

It is true that Mitty Beebe and her two little sisters, Millie and Jessie, died on Star Island in 1863. Their gravestones are in the island's cemetery. Mitty was seven when she died, Millie was four, and Jessie was two. They died from scarlet fever or another illness. Their father, the Reverend George Beebe, served as the island's minister.

Many people have claimed to see the ghosts of the Beebe sisters playing in the area near the cemetery. They say that the children run away or disappear when anyone approaches.

The chapel, which was built around 1800, also has a spooky history. Visitors sometimes hear singing coming from the chapel, but then find it to be empty. Others have said they've seen ghosts there.

The isles have been inhabited since the 1600s, but few people live there today. The University of New Hampshire runs a marine research center on Appledore Island, which is the largest of the isles. Visitors can make trips to Star Island on a ship from Portsmouth Harbor.

# GLOSSARY

**avast** – a sailor's term for stop.

**christen** – to name at baptism.

**eerie** – something mysterious or strange that sends a chill up the spine.

**hunch** – a strong feeling about something in the future.

**hymn** – a song that is sung in a religious service.

**nursery** – a child's bedroom.

**phantom** – something you can sense but doesn't actually exist.

**tragic** – something serious or unpleasant.

# WEB SITES

To learn more about the Star Island spirits, visit ABDO Group online at **www.abdopublishing.com**. Web sites about Star Island are featured on our Book Links page. These links are routinely monitored and updated to provide the most current information available.